First published in hardback in Great Britain by HarperCollins Children's Books in 2014

First published in paperback in 2015

10 9 8 7 6 5 4

ISBN: 978-0-00-758677-6

HarperCollins Children's Books is a division of HarperCollins Publishers Ltd.

Text and illustrations copyright © Kerr-Kneale Productions Ltd 2014

Visit our website at www.harpercollins.co.uk

Printed and bound in China

The Crocodile
Under the Bed

Judith Kerr

HarperCollins *Children's Books*

For the children next door:
Vanessa, Benedict, Tatum, Lulu,
James, Ludovico and Niccolo

Once there was a little boy called Matty, and he
was very sad. He was sad because he was sick.
He was too sick to go to the party, and it was a
very special party. It was a party for the Queen's
birthday, and there was going to be birthday
cake and a big slide.

Matty's mummy said, "Look who's here!
Grandpa has come to sit with you while we're out."
Matty said, "But I want to go to the party!"
Matty's mummy said, "We'll bring you back
some birthday cake."
Matty said, "But I want to go to the party!"
Matty's daddy said, "Look, here's a party blower
just like your sister's, so you can have a little
party all by yourself."

Matty said, "I don't want to have a little party all by myself.
And what if I need a drink while you're out?"
Matty's mummy said, "Grandpa will see to it."
Matty said, "Or what if I need to go to the loo?"
Matty's mummy said, "Grandpa will see to it."

Matty said, "Or what if there's a great big enormous
green crocodile hiding under my bed?"

Matty's mummy said, "Grandpa will see to it,"
and shut the door. Matty shouted, "I want to
go to the party!" But they had all gone.

It was very quiet after they'd gone.
Grandpa was quiet too.
Suddenly a voice said, "Want to go to a party?"
Matty said, "Who...?"

The crocodile said, "I'll fly you there."
Matty said, "But..."

The crocodile said, "Bring your party blower."
Matty said, "My blower...?"

The crocodile said, "Now blow!"
So Matty blew, and they flew out of the window
into the big open sky.

Matty said, "Are we going
to a special party?"
"Very special," said the crocodile.
"It's the King's birthday."
Matty said, "And will there be
a big slide?"
"Slides, rides and water glides,"
said the crocodile.
"They've got them all…

...and there's Chimpy.
He'll show you round."

"Glad you could come," said the King. "Have some birthday cake."

It was very good birthday cake.

"And now perhaps you'd like to try some of our rides," said the queen.

"Yes," said the king. "Start with the Great Rip Roarer."

"And then the Big Bouncer," said the queen.

"And a slide," said the king. "A slide on the Great Serpentine Winder."

"And finish with a lovely water glide on the Fat Flapper," said the queen. "Chimpy will show you."

"This way for the Great Rip Roarer,"
said Chimpy.

"Are you ready for your rip-roaring ride?"
"What's a rip-roaring ride?" said Matty.
"He rips through the jungle and roars," said Chimpy.
"Hold on tight."

It was a very good rip-roaring ride.

"And this is the Big Bouncer,"
said Chimpy.

"You can have one big bounce
or lots of little bounces."
"One big bounce, please," said Matty.
It was a very good big bounce.

"And now for your big slide," said Chimpy.
"It's a very special slide.
It is called the Great Serpentine Winder,
and there's a surprise at the end."

It was the best, biggest slide Matty had ever had,
and it finished on a fish.
"Welcome to the Fat Flapper," said Chimpy.
They had a lovely water glide.
But suddenly... "There's the crocodile," said Chimpy.
"I think it wants to take you home."

"Quick," said the crocodile.
"They're all leaving the party early.
We must have you back in bed before
your mummy and daddy get home."

When Matty's mummy and daddy got home
Matty was in bed just as they had left him.
"We've brought you back some birthday cake,"
said Matty's mummy. "I'm afraid it got a bit wet."

"But it was all horrible," said Matty's sister.
"Everything was wet, and we didn't see the queen,
and they said there would be a big slide,
but there was only a little tiny one for babies."
"So you see, you really didn't miss anything," said Matty's daddy.

"No," said Matty. "I didn't, did I?"